Don't Blow Your Top

A Look Inside Volcanoes

D1450993

by Anna Prokos

RED
CHAIR
•PRESS•

illustrated by
Elena Selivanova

Imagine That! books are produced and published by Red Chair Press

Red Chair Press LLC   PO Box 333   South Egremont, MA 01258-0333

www.redchairpress.com

FREE Lesson Plans from Lerner eSource
and at www.redchairpress.com

Publisher's Cataloging-In-Publication Data
(Prepared by The Donohue Group, Inc.)

Names: Prokos, Anna. | Selivanova, Elena, illustrator.
Title: Don't blow your top! : a look inside volcanoes / by Anna Prokos ; illustrated by Elena Selivanova.

Description: South Egremont, MA : Red Chair Press, [2017] | Imagine that! | Interest age level: 006-009.
    | Includes Fact File data, a glossary and references for additional reading. | Includes bibliographical
    references and index. | Summary: "Volcanoes are more than just fiery mountains spewing smoke and
    ash into the air. In this book readers will get a close-up look when these majestic mountains blow their
    tops. Readers learn about magma and lava flow, and how volcanoes form."-- Provided by publisher.

Identifiers: LCCN 2016934108 | ISBN 978-1-63440-148-7 (library hardcover) | ISBN 978-1-63440-154-8
    (paperback) | ISBN 978-1-63440-160-9 (ebook)

Subjects: LCSH: Volcanic eruptions--Juvenile literature. | Volcanoes--Juvenile literature. | Magmas--
    Juvenile literature. | Lava flows--Juvenile literature. CYAC: Volcanic eruptions. | Volcanoes.

Classification: LCC QE521.3 .P76 2017 (print) | LCC QE521.3 (ebook) | DDC 551.21--dc23

Copyright © 2017 Red Chair Press LLC
RED CHAIR PRESS, the RED CHAIR and associated logos are registered trademarks of
Red Chair Press LLC.

All rights reserved. No part of this book may be reproduced, stored in an information
or retrieval system, or transmitted in any form by any means, electronic, mechanical
including photocopying, recording, or otherwise without the prior written permission
from the Publisher. For permissions, contact info@redchairpress.com

Technical charts by Joe LeMonnier

Photo credits: Shutterstock, Inc

First Edition by:
Red Chair Press LLC   PO Box 333   South Egremont, MA 01258-0333

Printed in the United States of America
Distributed in the U.S. by Lerner Publisher Services. www.lernerbooks.com

1116 1P CGBS17

In 2010, a large volcano blasted in Iceland and the ash in the sky stopped airplanes from flying in Europe for weeks. In 2015, a different volcano began releasing hot fiery magma under an icecap. But this time, ash was limited. Eventually tourists were able to visit nearby to view the erupting volcano.

Hold on to your hat and let's imagine what it's like when these majestic mountains blow their tops!

TABLE OF CONTENTS

Kayla raced down the field. She dribbled the soccer ball around the other team. She set her sights on the goal. With one strong kick, the ball soared towards the net. The crowd cheered wildly!

Kayla had practiced all season long. She spent hours dribbling, kicking and running. She really wanted to score a goal for her team.

"Grrrr!" Kayla growled. "I should have scored that goal!" She threw her hands up in the air. She kicked the ground. She stormed off the field. Kayla was really angry.

Her team tried to cheer her up, but Kayla wouldn't listen. She got angrier and angrier. She clenched her fists. Her face turned bright red.

"That's ok," her teammates said. "The game isn't over. We'll get another shot!"

"Calm down, Kayla," her coach said softly. "Take some deep breaths. Don't blow your top like a volcano!"

Kayla tried to relax. She breathed slowly and counted to 10 to calm down. With each breath, she imagined she was on top of a volcano.

"Look out!" Kayla heard someone say. It didn't sound like her coach. She looked around and realized she wasn't on the soccer field anymore. She was on top of a mountain.

"It's going to blow its top!" the voice warned. A man with a yellow helmet and lots of ropes shook Kayla's hand.

"I'm Vin, a volcanologist. I study volcanoes like this one."

IT'S A FACT

Scientists use sensors and technology to monitor volcanoes and warn people when it might explode.

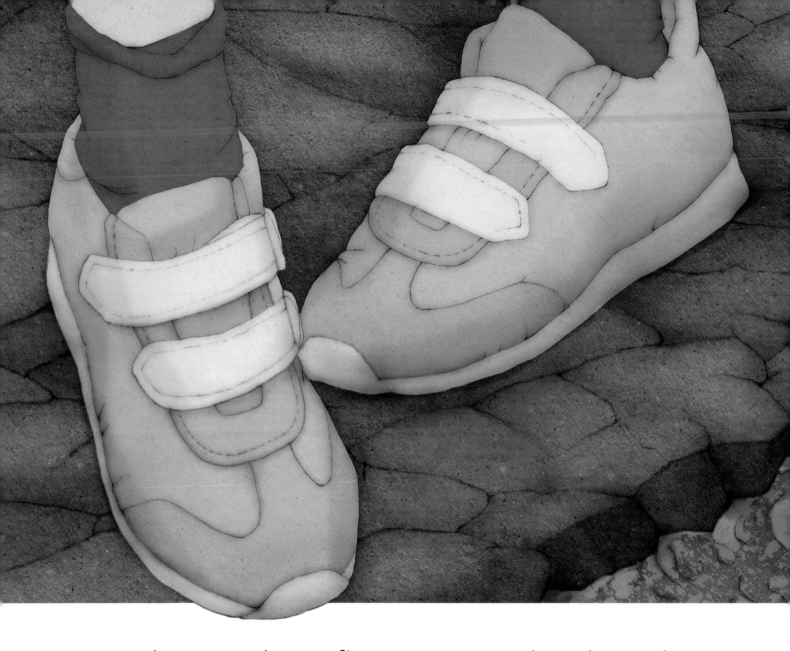

"That's a volcanic **fissure**," Vin explained. "And that red stuff is **magma**. It's rock that's been melted deep down in the earth. And now it's rising up to the surface."

"That's so cool!" Kayla said.

"Actually, it's so hot," Vin corrected. "Magma can be more than 2,000 degrees Fahrenheit (about 1,100 degrees Celsius). Don't get too close!"

"My coach says I blow my top like a volcano. Where's this volcano's top?" Kayla asked, looking around.

"We're standing on it," Vin said. "This is the summit crater. In just a few minutes, the bubbling magma will burst up from the magma chamber down below. All the pressure will throw the top of this crater into the air — along with red-hot magma."

Kayla's jaw dropped. "L-l-l-let's get out of here!" she exclaimed.

IT'S A FACT

There are volcanoes on the oceans floors and under icecaps and glaciers, as in Iceland.

IT'S A FACT

Volcanoes act like giant safety valves on a pressure cooker. They release pressure from inside Earth.

"Hold on tight!" Vin said, as he hooked her to his belt. The two rappelled down the mountain.

As they moved down the ropes, they heard a loud rumble. "That was not my stomach growling," Kayla said.

"That's the sound of rocks melting and moving inside the eruption column," Vin said. "The rocks and the magma are bubbling up to the top."

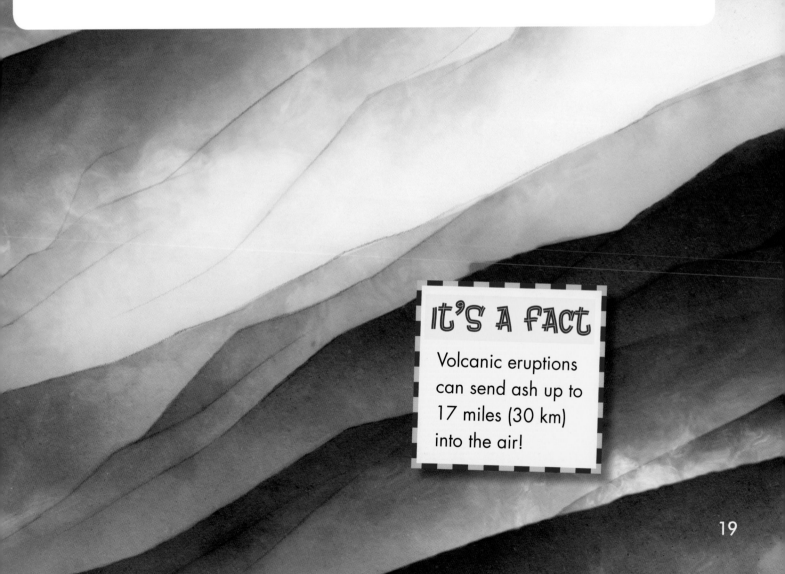

"It's a good thing we're heading down," Kayla said, trembling. Suddenly, she heard a loud hiss. A blast of smoky steam burst out behind her.

"As magma moves towards the top, pressure builds inside the volcano. Hot gas escapes through cracks, or vents, in the mountain," Vin explained.

IT'S A FACT

Volcanic eruptions can send ash up to 17 miles (30 km) into the air!

Finally, they reached the bottom. Kayla felt the ground tremble beneath her feet.

"Take cover!" Vin shouted. He and Kayla ran away from the mountain. A loud boom echoed through the air.

"It blew its top!" Kayla yelled. Suddenly, they were caught in a storm of rocks and fire! They dodged **pyroclastic** rocks. They swerved around flaming rain.

IT'S A FACT

Some eruption flows move slowly. Others move very fast like an avalanche. All are extremely dangerous.

A red river streamed down the mountain. It was creeping up behind them!

"A lava flow!" Vin called out. "Magma that escapes from a volcano is called lava. Lava can flow quickly or slowly. Over time, it cools and hardens to form more land or another volcano. But that can take hundreds of years."

"I'm not going to stick around for that!" Kayla told him.

"Are you ready to get back in the game?" Kayla heard a familiar voice ask. She exhaled slowly and turned to face her coach.

"I'm ready!" she said. "And I promise I won't blow my top like a volcano—
because THAT is very scary!"

Kayla high-fived her teammates and they ran to the soccer field. The crowd cheered — and Kayla knew this time she would keep her cool.

Don't Blow Your Top

Cross section through a volcano

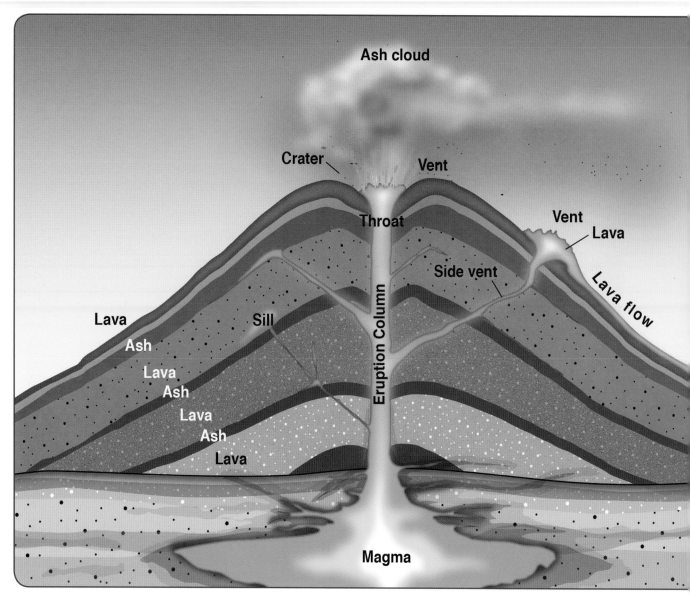

Ash cloud

Crater

Vent

Throat

Vent

Lava

Side vent

Lava flow

Lava

Sill

Ash

Eruption Column

Lava

Ash

Lava

Ash

Lava

Magma

ash: small fragments of lava or rock

crater: mouth of a volcano, surrounds a larger vent

sill: flat rock formed when magma hardens inside a crack in the volcano

vent: an opening through which volcanic pressure escapes

27

Ring of Fire

Did you know volcanoes can be found all around the world? Most are located in a line around the edges of the Pacific Ocean. About 75% or 3 of every 4 volcanoes on Earth are located in this Ring of Fire.

The Earth's outer crust is made up of 7 large and 12 smaller movable slabs of rock called **tectonic plates**. The plates sit on a layer of **mantle**, made up of hot liquid. These plates are always sliding around at very slow speed. The Pacific plate under the ocean is the largest of all. When it collides with another plate it might cause an earthquake. When it slides under another plate, hot molten rock, or magma, may rise to the surface. This results in hot fiery volcanoes.

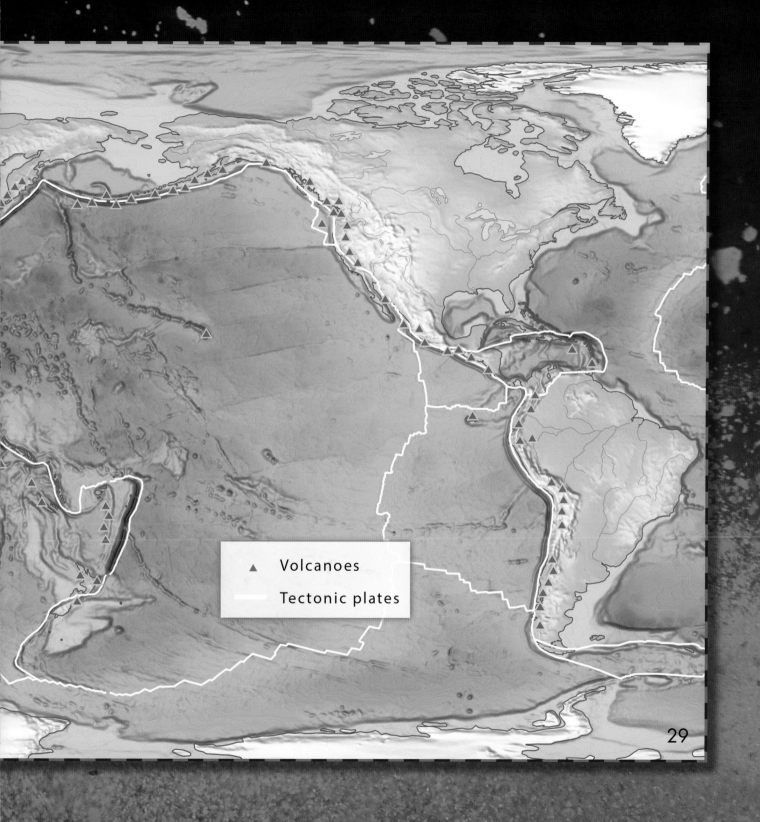

Volcanoes

Tectonic plates

Volcanoes Around the World

Scientists now believe the **Tamu Massif** in the Pacific Ocean (1,000 miles/1,600 km east of Japan) is the largest volcano on Earth. This shield volcano spreads out as large as Kansas. It was only discovered in 2013.

Mauna Kea in Hawaii is the world's tallest volcano. It is one of five on the state's big island of Hawaii. The base of the volcano is over 19,000 feet (6,000 meters) below sea level on the ocean floor. If measured from the base to the summit, the volcano is over 33,000 feet tall, making it Earth's tallest mountain.

Kilimanjaro is Africa's most famous volcano. This cone-shaped stratovolcano towers over Tanzania and Kenya.

On the border of Argentina and Chile in the Andes Mountains lies **Ojos del Salado**. At over 22,000 feet (6,880 meters) high this volcano has the world's highest summit elevation (meaning all above sea level).

Science Says . . .
The biggest eruptions in history happened in:

- Yellowstone (U.S.) about 2.2 million years ago
- Tambora, Indonesia in 1815
- Baitoushan (China-N.Korea) about 1050
- Kikai, Japan about 4350 B.C.
- Crater Lake, Oregon (U.S.) about 4895 B.C.

Source: Oregon State University

A rock formed from cooled lava.

Words to Keep

fissure: a narrow opening or crack in Earth's rocky surface.

magma: hot, melted or molten rock.

mantle: the layer beneath Earth's crust.

pyroclastic: coming from volcanoes.

tectonic plates: slabs of continental or ocean crust that sit on the Earth's mantle

Learn More at the Library

Books

Branley, Franklyn M. *Volcanoes* (Let's Find Out Science). Harper Collins, 2008.

Furgang, Kathy. *Everything Volcanoes and Earthquakes.* National Geographic Children's Books, 2013.

Oxlade, Chris. *Volcanoes.* Heinemann-Raintree, 2014.

Web Sites

Discovery Kids
http://discoverykids.com/games/volcano-explorer/

National Geographic Kids
http://www.ngkids.co.uk/science-and-nature/Volcano-Facts

Index